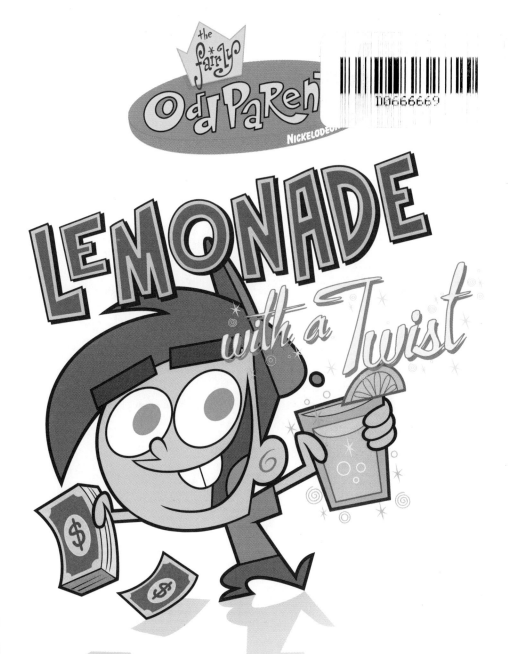

the Fairly OddParents

NICKELODEON

LEMONADE with a Twist

by Steven Banks   illustrated by Victoria Miller
based on the teleplay by Jack Thomas

Ready-to-Read

Simon Spotlight/Nickelodeon
New York   London   Toronto   Sydney   Singapore

Based on the TV series *The Fairly OddParents*®
created by Butch Hartman as seen on Nickelodeon®

SIMON SPOTLIGHT
An imprint of Simon & Schuster Children's Publishing Division
1230 Avenue of the Americas, New York, New York 10020

Manufactured in the United States of America

First Edition
2 4 6 8 10 9 7 5 3 1

Library of Congress Cataloging-in-Publication Data
Banks, Steven.
Lemonade with a twist! / by Steven Banks ; based on the teleplay by
Jack Thomas.—1st ed.
p. cm.—(Ready-to-read ; #2)
"Based on the TV series The Fairly OddParents® created by
Butch Hartman as seen on Nickelodeon®."
Summary: With the unwitting help of his fairy godparents, Timmy makes
a magical lemonade that grants drinkers' wishes, with unexpected results.
ISBN 0-689-86321-7
[1. Fairies—Fiction. 2. Wishes—Fiction.] I. Thomas, Jack. II. Title.
III. Series.
PZ7.B22637 Le 2004
[E]—dc21
2003010013

Crash Nebula on Ice was coming to
the Dimmsdale Dimm-a-Dome!
"We **must** get tickets!" cried A.J.
"No problem," said Timmy calmly.

After his friends left
Timmy called for tickets.
But the show was
completely sold out!

The next day A.J. and Chester
were mad at Timmy.
"Do not worry," said Timmy.
"I can still get tickets."
Timmy took a deep breath
and walked into the boys' bathroom.

"Welcome to Francis's Toilet
of Tickets," Francis said, grunting
as he popped out of the toilet.
Timmy asked him for three tickets to
Crash Nebula on Ice.

But Francis wanted fifteen
hundred dollars!
The boys did not have the money.
"Too bad," Francis said, sneering
as he slid back into the toilet.

Back at home Timmy tried
to wish for tickets. But Cosmo
and Wanda said that it would
be against **Da Rules** to take
the tickets away from someone else.
Timmy had to **earn** the money!

Timmy opened a lemonade stand.

His mother was his first customer.

She took a sip and

immediately spat it out.

"This is horrible!" she cried.

Timmy's baby-sitter, Vicky,

set up a lemonade stand

right next to Timmy's.

Mrs. Turner decided to try

Vicky's lemonade.

Vicky opened a trapdoor.

A boy was making lemonade

in a dark pit.

"One lemonade!" yelled Vicky.

The boy quickly made some

and Timmy's mother took a sip.

"Yummy!" she cried.

Timmy had to make his
lemonade better.
He tried adding cheese,
taco sauce, and peas.
But it was worse than before!

Wanda said Timmy should wish
for sweeter lemonade.
Cosmo then took off his socks and
dipped them in Timmy's glass.
"I said **sweeter**, not sweatier!"
Wanda said with a frown.

Timmy loved the new lemonade.

"I wish I had a whole

pitcher of it!" he yelled.

Before Cosmo and Wanda

could grant Timmy's wish,

a pitcher of lemonade appeared.

A.J. tested the lemonade.

"This is great!" he shouted. "I wish **everybody** knew about it!"

Suddenly a news van pulled up and Chet Ubetcha jumped out.

"Hello, Dimmsdale!" he announced.

"Everybody should try

this lemonade!"

Soon hundreds of people

lined up at the stand.

"At this rate we will **own**
Crash Nebula!" said A.J.
as he counted their money.
Then Timmy saw that they were
almost out of lemonade.
"Man the fort," he instructed.

Timmy ran into the garage.

Cosmo was pedaling on a bike

to make more fairy sweat

for the lemonade.

"Getting . . . tired,"

Cosmo said, moaning.

"Less talkie! More sweatie!"

ordered Timmy.

Outside a little boy gulped
down some lemonade. He wished that
his old dog Speedy was with him.
Then Speedy appeared.

"Wow!" said Timmy.

"When people drink Cosmo's sweat
their wishes are granted!"

Timmy's dad tried the lemonade.

"I wish I did not have to go to work.

I could drink this all day!"

Then a giant lizard gobbled down

Mr. Turner's office building!

"Cool!" said Mr. Turner, grinning.

Suddenly everybody's wishes were

coming true. Mrs. Turner wished

that Mr. Turner was stronger!

Chet Ubetcha wished
that he was
twenty feet tall!

Then the giant lizard stomped
toward Timmy's house! **ROAR!**

Timmy raced to his garage.

He found Cosmo slumped over

on the bike.

"Everybody's wishes are

coming true!" yelled Timmy.

"What are we going to do?"

Timmy squeezed the last bit of sweat
into a glass. He had enough to make
just one more glass of lemonade.
ROAR! The lizard had arrived!

Timmy grabbed the last glass.

He took a sip as the lizard

was about to attack.

Timmy wished that the lizard

was two inches tall.

POOF! The lizard shrank.

Timmy took another sip and
wished that everything was
back to normal.

But now Timmy had no money.
He could not buy the tickets
to **Crash Nebula on Ice!**

There was still a little lemonade
left in the glass.
He saw the boy
who had worked for Vicky
crawl out of the pit.
"I **must** have something to drink!"
he begged. Timmy gave him
the last bit of lemonade.

"I wish my father were here,"
said the boy. Suddenly a car
pulled up. Out stepped
Doug Dimmsdale, owner of the
Dimmsdale Dimm-a-Dome.
Timmy had found Doug's
long-lost son, Dale!

"How can I repay you?"

asked Mr. Dimmsdale.

Timmy wanted three tickets

to **Crash Nebula on Ice.**

Mr. Dimmsdale said it was sold out,

but there was **one** way they

could see the show. . . .

That night Timmy and his friends

saw **Crash Nebula on Ice.**

"I told you I would get you in,"

said Timmy, grinning.

Then the boys got back to work.

"Get your ice-cold lemonade!"